W9-AHH-503

Atheneum Books for Young Readers
An imprint of Simon & Schuster Children's Publishing Division
1230 Avenue of the Americas
New York, New York 10020
Text copyright © 1998 by Campbell Geeslin
Illustrations copyright © 1998 by Petra Mathers
Book design by Ann Bobco
The text of this book is set in Triplex Serif Extrabold.
The illustrations are rendered in watercolor, ink, and colored pencil.
First Edition
Printed in Hong Kong
10 9 8 7 6 5 4 3 2 1

Library of Congress Cataloging-in-Publication Data
Geeslin, Campbell.
On Ramón's farm : five tales of Mexico / by Campbell Geeslin ;
illustrated by Petra Mathers.—1st ed.
p. cm.
"An Anne Schwartz book."
Summary: The animals that Ramón tends on his family's farm in Mexico include
sheep that weep when they're shorn and a goat that climbs to the top of a windmill.
Includes some Spanish words with pronunciation.
ISBN 0-689-81134-9
[1. Domestic animals—Fiction. 2. Farm life—Fiction. 3. Animal sounds—Fiction.
4. Mexico—Fiction. 5. Spanish language—Vocabulary.] I. Mathers, Petra, ill. II. Title.
PZ7.G258450n 1998
[E]—dc20
96-20034

On Ramón's Farm

Five Tales of Mexico

By Campbell Geeslin

Illustrated by Petra Mathers

An Anne Schwartz Book
ATHENEUM BOOKS FOR YOUNG READERS

For all the boys: Seth, Ned, Gary, and Max
— C. G.

For Jeff in heaven
— P. M.

Ramón lives on a farm in Mexico.

All day his mamá is busy weaving, so Ramón's job is to take care of the animals. Ramón speaks Spanish. The animals talk like this:

Quiquiriqui!

Me-me-me!

Me-e-e!

Oing-oing!

Je-ja!

As Ramón does his chores, he likes to make up rhymes about the funny ways that the animals act.

LAS OVEJAS

una alfombrilla (OON-uh al-foam-BREE-yah): **a rug**

me-e-e (MAY-ay-ay): **baa-ah-ah**

Montaña Grande (moan-TAHN-yah GRAHN-day): **Big Mountain**

las ovejas (LAS oh-VEH-hahs): **the sheep**

un sarape (OON sa-RAH-pay): **a shawl**

At the foot of Montaña Grande, Ramón watches after his mamá's ovejas.

There are only two: Pepita and Luisa. They are twin sisters.
One spring day, Ramón cuts Pepita's wool so that his
mamá can make un sarape.

Pepita cries and cries.

Ramón cuts Luisa's wool so that
his mamá can make una alfombrilla.

Luisa cries and cries.

The other boys and girls who look after the flocks on Montaña Grande shear their ovejas, too.

Pepita's eyes turn red from weeping. Luisa's sobs grow louder.

Ramón asks Pepita and Luisa, "If I tie ribbons around your necks, will you stop crying?"

"Me-e-e!" they say.

Pepita's ribbon is pink, and Luisa's ribbon is orange.
Pepita and Luisa admire themselves in the river.
    When the other ovejas see how pretty Pepita and Luisa
look, they cry and cry until . . .

. . . their boys and girls give them ribbons, too.

Ramón thinks all las ovejas look as if they are going
to a party. He makes up a rhyme:

> Ovejas always want to be
> Like the others that they see.

EL GALLO

adiós (ah-dee-OSE): **good-bye**

amigo (ah-MEE-go): **friend**

dos (dose): **two**

el gallo (ELL GA-yoe): **the rooster**

mira (MEER-ah): **look**

pío-pío (PEE-oh PEE-oh): **peep-peep**

quiquiriqui (key-key-REE-key): **cock-a-doodle-do**

uno (OO-no): **one**

Ramón's mamá has a new tin bucket. Ramón fills it
with water and leaves it by the kitchen door.

When el gallo sees it, he perches
on the rim and takes a sip
of the cool water.

Mira!

Another gallo is staring up
at him from inside.

El gallo sings,
"Oh, what a fine doodle-do you are!"

All day el gallo struts around the yard, returning
to visit his quiet new amigo. Whenever he looks, his
amigo is right there, giving him smiles.

But one day, his amigo in the bucket does not smile.

Instead, he spreads his great wings and ruffles his magnificent tail feathers.

El gallo is angry.

"What a silly doodle-do you have become!" he says. "Why don't you fold up your fancy feathers and go home?"

He marches away in disgust.

Still, el gallo can't help coming back. Now the big bird in the bucket rolls his eyes and threatens el gallo with his sharp beak and talons.

El gallo flies at him.

BANG!

SPLASH!

CRASH!

The bucket turns over and all the water spills out.
"Adiós, my old amigo," croaks el gallo.

El gallo's beak is
dented. In the morning
when he wakes up,
his quiquiriquí
won't work. He cheeps,
"Pío-pío!"

But he struts around Ramón's farm
more proudly than ever before.

Ramón's rhyme goes:
  Uno gallo? What a glorious sight!
  Dos gallos? Ay, what a fight!

EL CABRITO

el cabrito (ELL kah-BREE-toe): **the young goat**

me-me-me (meh-meh-meh): **meh-eh-eh**

pequeño mío (pe-KAYN-yo MEE-oh): **my little one**

**One night Ramón is awakened
by loud sounds on the roof.**

He climbs out his window to look.

In the moonlight he sees el cabrito jumping around on the roof tiles. "Me-me-me!"
"Come down from there!" Ramón says. "You'll wake Mamá."
But el cabrito trots up to the highest point
and jumps gaily up and down.

His hoofs go,

CRASH!

CLATTER!

CRASH!

Ramón gets his ladder and climbs onto the roof. He pulls el cabrito down and ties him to the mesquite tree.

The next morning Ramón finds
el cabrito up high in the mesquite,
looking this way and that, all excited.
Ramón pulls him down and ties him
to the windmill.

In the afternoon, el cabrito is on top of the windmill.

He is spinning round and round, growing dizzier and dizzier.

But he is smiling.
Ramón brings el cabrito down.

"Oh, pequeño mío!" he says, sighing. "You are more trouble than all the other animals put together. Why are you always climbing?"

But el cabrito has already trotted off, dragging Ramón's
ladder behind him.

Ramón makes up a rhyme that goes:
The sky must hold some mysteries
That only el cabrito sees.

EL BURRO

el burro (ELL BOOR-row): **the donkey**

je-ja (HAY-hah): **hee-haw**

la plaza (LA PLAZ-ah): **the marketplace**

una roca (OON-uh ROW-kah): **a rock**

Ramón gathers sticks. He stacks them high onto his burro, Pedro, and ties them with a rope.

Ramón will take the firewood to sell in la plaza.

"Let's go, Pedro," he says.

Pedro takes one step forward and two steps back.

"No, no!" says Ramón, kicking at Pedro lightly. "We're going to la plaza."

Pedro takes one step forward and two steps back.

"Stop that!" Ramón yells.

Now he grabs Pedro's ears and pulls them. "La plaza is *that* way!"

Pedro takes one step forward and two steps back.

Ramón gives up and sits on una roca to think.

Down from the sky flies a big crow.

"I'll help you with that burro if you'll feed me,"
the crow says and then whispers something in Ramón's ear.

Ramón smiles and gives the bird a big ear of corn.
Ramón puts a blindfold on Pedro and turns him
around. "Now, my stubborn burro," he says. "Let's go!"

Pedro takes one step forward and two steps back.

All the way down to la plaza—
one step forward, two steps back,
one step forward, two steps back.

The villagers have never
seen a dancing burro before.
They clap their hands and cheer.
"Je-ja!" says Pedro.

Ramón's rhyme goes:
A burro can't be pulled or kicked,
But dances into town if tricked!

FRUTAS
Y
LEGUMBRES

EL CERDO

el cerdo (ELL SEHR-doh): **the pig**

oing-oing (AW-ing AW-ing): **oink-oink**

Olé! (oh-LAY!): **Well done!**

señor (sen-YOR): **mister**

el toro (ELL TOR-oh): **the bull**

Ramón likes to pretend to be a bullfighter. He borrows his mamá's red apron and says to el cerdo, "When I wave my cape at you, chase me, and I will leap out of the way."

"Oing-oing," says el cerdo in a pitiful voice. "I'm much too hungry. I need something to eat."

So Ramón gives el cerdo three ears of corn, and el cerdo gobbles them down,

crunch,

crunch,

crunch!

Ramón waves the red apron at el cerdo and cries, "Toro! Toro!"
But el cerdo just stands and blinks.

"I'm sorry," he whines,
"but I'm still starving."

Ramón pulls the thorns from a big prickly pear. El
cerdo smacks his lips and swallows the fruit whole,

slurp!

Again, Ramón waves his apron, and el cerdo moans,
"That pear was good, but I'm still weak from hunger."

Ramón takes a stick and beats the mesquite branches.

All its beans tumble to the ground,

and el cerdo gulps them down, smacking his lips,
yum, yum, yum!

Ramón says, "Come on now and chase me."
El cerdo sinks into the dust with a happy smile.
"Oh please, señor. I'm much too full. Go away."
And he begins to snore,

zezz,

zezz,

zezz.

Ramón sighs. "I'll have to practice with the wind," he says.

"Olé! Olé!" cries the crow in the mesquite tree.

Ramón's rhyme goes:
    Don't ask el cerdo to be a bull
    Especially when his belly's full.

buenos sueños (boo-WAY-noss SWAYN-yoss): **sweet dreams**

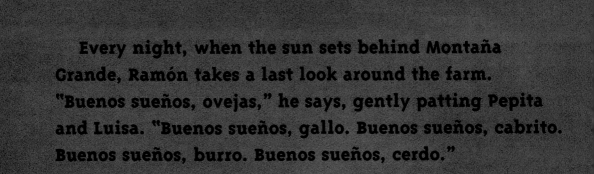

**Every night, when the sun sets behind Montaña
Grande, Ramón takes a last look around the farm.
"Buenos sueños, ovejas," he says, gently patting Pepita
and Luisa. "Buenos sueños, gallo. Buenos sueños, cabrito.
Buenos sueños, burro. Buenos sueños, cerdo."**

And a chorus of animals says,

Me-e-e!

Oing-oing!

Me-me-me!

Quiquiriqui!

Je-ja!

just before they all go to sleep.